Little Bear's
BIG ADVENTURE

Illustrated by Clare Fennell
Written by Sarah Phillips

make
believe
ideas

One fine winter morning
Little Bear awoke from a long sleep.

"It must be time to get up," he said to himself.

"Look how bright the light is!"

He put
on his
scarf,
picked up
his **hat**,
and
tiptoed
past
Mommy
Bear's
bed.

Little Bear opened the door
and was dazzled by the
shimmering scene.

The trees were wearing
white, fluffy coats
and the ground was as
cold as ice cream.

the Bear
ResiDenCe

do Not
Disturb

"This must
be snow!"

thought Little Bear.

"How strange

it looks!

I'm going

exploring!"

As Little Bear **set off** towards the trees, he sang to himself:

"I'm walking through the forest,

I'm a very *brave* bear!

I'll climb a tree

and *see* what I *see*!

I'm not scared!"

From the top of the Big Pine,

Little Bear gazed at the snow-clad forest,

sparkling like

a million crystals

in the sunshine.

The forest

looked different.

It even smelled different!

Little Bear jumped down
from the Big Pine.

Wheee

He landed on his bottom
and began to slide.

He slipped down the slope, faster and faster, until THUD,

he hit a soft, white bank of snow.

"Wow!" he cried.

"That was amazing!

I'll do it again!"

And he climbed back up the slope, singing:

"I'm walking through the forest,
I'm a very brave bear!
Watch me go
on the slippery snow!
I'm not scared!"

Sliding was fun,

but after a while,

Little Bear began to feel lonely.

"I know," he said to himself.

"I'll make a Snow Bear friend."   So he got busy, pushing, piling, and

...olling the snow, singing as he worked:

"I'm walking through the forest, I'm a very brave bear!
I'll burrow and dig to build something big! I'm not scared!"

"HELLO!"

said Little Bear

in his biggest voice.

But Snow Bear did not reply.

"What's all that noise?"

said a sweet voice

from the trees,

and with a

"tweet, tweet, tweet,"

Red Bird appeared.

"What a great Snow Bear!" said Red Bird.

"But he needs some hair. Wait here!"

Before Little Bear
could say a word,
Red Bird flew off
and returned
with a mouthful of moss.
"Thank you, Red Bird!"
said Little Bear.

"Snow Bear's perfect now . . .
but all that work has
made me hot!"

"Try this,"
said Red Bird, handing
him a **spiky** icicle.
"It's a real **tweet!**"

Red Bird and Little Bear
licked icicles until they
were no longer thirsty.

"Thank you, Red Bird!" said Little Bear.

"Would you like to come sliding with me?"

Taking Red Bird on his arm, Little Bear sat down and

whoosh!

Down the slope they went, slipping, sliding, skidding, and spinning

all the way

to the stream.

"WOW!"
shouted Little Bear.

"TWEET!"
cried Red Bird.

Little Bear stepped onto the ice
and found that he could skate!

"Look at this!"

he called to Red Bird

as he spun round and round

and sang at the

top of his voice:

"I'm walking through the forest,
I'm a very brave bear!
Watch me go
on the slippery snow!
I'm not scared!"

Little Bear skated along the stream and onto the pond, twirling round and round in circles until . . .

THUMP, he fell on his bottom.

OUCH!

Little Bear was upset.

He felt dizzy and cold and lost.

Two big tears rolled
down Little Bear's face.

"Come on," said Red Bird.

"You're a
very brave bear,
remember?"

Little Bear looked at Red Bird. He couldn't manage a smile,

but he did start to sing very quietly:

"I'm walking through the forest
and I'm a very brave bear!
To find the way back,
I'll follow my tracks!
I'm only a little scared!"

Slowly and carefully,
Little Bear walked back **around** the pond,

along the stream, up the hill, and past Snow Bear,

singing
as he went:

"I've walked through the forest,
I'm a very brave bear!
My home's in sight,
I can see the light!
I'm no longer scared!"

Mommy Bear was standing
at the door of the house.
"Where have you been, Little Bear?
It's not time for us to get up.
It's much too cold.
Come inside this minute."

"Yes, Mommy," said Little Bear.

"Bye-bye, Red Bird,

and thank you!"

"Tweet, tweet!" said Red Bird.

Mommy Bear gave Little Bear a **hug** and **tucked** him into bed.

"We need another **long** sleep," she said.

"When we wake up, the snow will have **melted**

and it will be **spring**."

Little Bear felt **tired** and **happy**.

He closed his eyes

and Mommy Bear sang:

"You've been walking through the forest,
you're my brave Little Bear!
I'll say good night, then you'll sleep tight,
until the spring is here!"

And before Mommy Bear could say another word,

Little Bear was fast asleep.